A REGULAR ROLLING NOAH

A REGULAR

By George Ella Lyon

Aladdin Books

Macmillan Publishing Company New York   Collier Macmillan Canada Toronto
Maxwell Macmillan International Publishing Group New York Oxford Singapore Sydney

ROLLING NOAH

Illustrated by Stephen Gammell

For my father
and in memory of my grandfather
who made this journey — G.E.L.

Now I'd never seen a train before today, but I've heard its whistle down at the mouth of the hollow.

The Creeches are taking it to Canada,
moving their whole farm.
They've hired me to go along
and tend the stock. I can do that.
I'm a good hand with animals.

"I'm afraid we're plumb full,"
Mrs. Creech calls from the wagon.
"You be the cow's tail."

Bedding and seeds and plows,
pot vessels and young'uns —
we load them into the train
and it shrieking and steaming.

Hay and feed in the boxcar,
then the chickens and guineas,
Rosie and her calf.

Only the mare balks.
''Get along there, Bad Patch!''
I have to throw my nightshirt
over her head.

All day we ride
winding through mountains.

At dark I milk Rosie,
make a supper of milk and bread.
The train clatters along
farther and farther and farther.

In the morning it stops.
Someone slides the door open.
At first I see just the railyard,
steam like fog in the hollow.
But then I feel what's happened.

We've run out of mountains.
Sky right down to your ankles.
Big wind might blow you away.

I gather eggs in my basket
aiming to trade with the hoboes
for breakfast.

Mr. Creech said I'd find them
at the fence or the edge of the yard.
Sure enough, there they are.

"Pardon me, mister.
I'm a Gabbard from Pathfork, Kentucky.
Could you take fresh eggs and milk
for coffee and the use of your fire?"

They trade,
ask me some questions.
I tell them about the boxcar.
"A regular rolling Noah," one says.
I don't mind.

They talk.
I forget time.
Then the whistle! the whistle!

I leap tracks and signals
and catch the boxcar handle
just as the wheels start to turn.

I sweep out the straw
and put down fresh.
I build nest boxes for the fowl.

Bad Patch I have to coddle
but Rosie stands as steady
as she did in her own field.
The calf I call Mossy.

Night wind whips through the slats
but I wrap up in my blanket
and bury myself in the hay
down between Rosie and Bad Patch.

Finally we arrive.
Strange place to draw up to —
land flat as a griddle.

I've cleaned and combed the mare,
doctored the cow's eye.
No point in me going farther.
We fit the wagon together
and load it. I say goodbye.

Mr. Creech gave me my ticket
as pay.   I'm riding in style
on a fine horsehair seat
among folks loud as my guineas.

World's a big affair.
I'm going to tell them in Pathfork:
Be glad you have these mountains
to call home.

First Aladdin Books edition 1991

Text copyright © 1986 by George Ella Lyon
Illustrations copyright © 1986 by Stephen Gammell

Aladdin Books
Macmillan Publishing Company
866 Third Avenue
New York, NY 10022
Collier Macmillan Canada, Inc.
1200 Eglinton Avenue East
Suite 200
Don Mills, Ontario M3C 3N1
Printed in USA
A hardcover edition of *A Regular Rolling Noah* is available from Bradbury Press, an affiliate of Macmillan Publishing Company.
1 2 3 4 5 6 7 8 9 10

Library of Congress Cataloging-in-Publication Data
Lyon, George Ella, 1949-
A regular rolling Noah/George Ella Lyon; illustrated by Stephen Gammell. — 1st Aladdin Books ed.
p.   cm.
Summary: The adventures of a young boy hired to shepherd a boxcar of farm animals from Kentucky to Canada.
ISBN 0-689-71449-1
[1. Voyages and travels — Fiction. 2. Domestic animals — Fiction. 3. Railroads — Trains — Fiction.] I. Gammell, Stephen, ill.
II. Title.
[PZ7.L9954Re   1991]
[E] — dc20   90–39984   CIP   AC